Stepbrother FRAT

Stepbrother Frat

Stephanie Brother

© 2023 (Second edition, enhanced and expanded with 6k more words of steamy romance)
© 2015 (First edition)

All Rights Reserved. This book or any portion thereof may not be reproduced or used in any manner whatsoever without the express permission of the publisher except for the use of brief quotations in a book review.

This book is a work of fiction. Any resemblance to persons, living or dead, or places, events or locations is purely coincidental. The characters are all productions of the author's imagination.

Please note that this work is intended only for adults over the age of 18 and all characters represented as 18 or over.

Print Edition

Contents

1	1
2	7
3	13
4	33
5	37
6	53
7	61
8	69
9	87
Also by Stephanie Brother	95
Excerpt from BIG 3	97
About the Author	117

1

Confusion filled me as I blinked my eyes open.

Where am I?

A quick glance down confirmed that I was fine: still fully dressed, phew. But for some reason, a sheet covered my entire body—including my head. Carefully, I inched it down my nose and peeked around the unfamiliar room. Red and gold decorations adorned the shelves. Deep crimson wallpaper spanned the walls; gleaming, stenciled Greek letters reading: Zeta Phi Pi.

Shit, I'm in the Zee Phi frat house!

The pounding in my ribcage sped up. My mind told me it couldn't be *too* bad since my stepbrother, Derek Sawyer, is a Zeta, but for the next couple of weeks, no one was safe. Not even Derek could protect me.

Yesterday afternoon, Callie Brooks, president of the Xi Nu Chi sorority announced that the Greek community would be participating in a new game. Killer, she called it. Each member would have a target from a different sorority or fraternity and would have to 'kill' them through writing on their body with a Sharpie. Whoever you killed would have to give you their Kandi—a bracelet strung in their house's colors—and give you the name of their target. The person with the most bracelets wins a date with any Greek of their choosing.

I wasn't planning on participating, but my sorority sister Darcy said it would be a great way to meet the other Greeks on campus. Something about expanding outside of our Tau Beta Mu sisterhood to meet genuine people... And maybe cute guys. Then we decided to celebrate with a glass of wine or three. I don't remember. But somehow, I ended up in my stepbrother's frat house. I looked at my left arm. Purple and white beads firmly slowed the circulation around my wrist. *Still alive. For now.*

Pulling out my sleek new phone, I opened the Messenger app.

Me: Darcy, what the hell? Why am I at the Zeta house?

Within seconds, Darcy replied with a string of laugh-crying emojis and the text, "You don't remember? You followed your brother there and refused to come home with me."

Cheeks flaming, I shot upright on the hardwood floor. *I followed Derek here? Why?* Well, there was one reason why. One obvious reason. Ever since our parents got hitched when I was sixteen, I was drawn to him like a magnet. But at the same time, I had always been extra careful in not revealing how I felt about him because I knew he would never look at me the same way again.

Muffled voices grew louder. I slipped my phone into my pocket and quietly lowered myself back down. Fortunately, I had the couch as a shield. I wiped my clammy palms on my jeans and steadied my breathing.

"Darcy? Yeah, she's alright. A little bit of a ditz," one of the voices said.

"What about her friend though? The chubby one? What's her name...." He snapped his fingers as if trying to remember. "Karla! That's it."

"Dude, shut up. That's Derek's sister," the other replied in a loud whisper.

Tears stung the corners of my eyes. *So that's how they saw me. The chubby one.*

"Oops. Sorry, I meant… The one with the ass!" Both guys erupted into laughter as the front door slammed shut.

Feeling humiliated, I scavenged for my purse. There was no hesitation as I rushed to the front door, the tears freely streaming down my face.

The first person I saw when I finally got into the sorority house was Darcy. She blanched when she spotted me.

"Hey," she said softly, her voice tinged with concern. "What's wrong? They didn't…did they?" She was already gasping in shock, as if I'd said yes. Good old Darcy, always assuming the worst.

"No." I almost laughed at the thought of any of the Zeta brothers being interested in me after what I just witnessed. "Nothing like that. I just overheard them talking and they were being jerks, that's all."

"Oh," she sighed in relief. "Well, whatever. Screw them. They're all ass hats anyway."

I giggled. I had only been initiated into Tau Beta Mu two months ago, but I already knew that I could trust Darcy to cheer me up when I was down.

"Anyways," she started excitedly. "The Tabbies just got invited to the Zeta's mixer this Friday! I have no idea what I'm going to wear. We should go shopping!"

For a split second, I was really excited, but then reality weighed down on me. I shook my head. "I'm not going, Darce."

"Why not? It's the first mixer we've been invited to this term! It's *your* first mixer, period!"

"I know, but I don't think they like me, Darcy. I wouldn't feel welcomed there."

"Don't be stupid, your brother's a Zeta. Of course, you'd be welcomed."

"He's my *step*brother, and anyway that doesn't mean anything. You didn't hear them today."

She looked sad for a moment, then she shrugged. "Well, you know where it is and where I'll be if you change your mind. I hope you do—this is a great way to get to know people!"

"You keep saying that. But I'm starting to think Greek life was a mistake; I don't belong here."

Turning serious, Darcy firmly grabbed my shoulders and shook me. "Don't ever say that, okay? You're our sister. You belong here as much as any of us. Now, as Spirit Chair, I demand that you go to your room and write down twenty reasons why you're amazing. Right. Now. Go!"

Shaking my head at her, I sulked back to my room. Not to write a list, but so I could mope some more. Enough moping would make everything better, right?

As I read the Facebook Event invite for Friday's mixer, I thought about it some more. On the one hand, it would be a great way to prove how awesome I am to all of the asshole Zeta brothers. On the other hand, I didn't ever want to see any of them again. Knowing that I was someone else's killer target and likely wouldn't be able to outrun them didn't help. *Add that to the list of reasons to mock you*, I berated myself. Then shaking my head hard, I forced myself to snap out of it—and to write down twenty reasons why I'm amazing.

2

I readjusted my backpack as I walked across campus to my 8:30 AM Calculus class. Why I had to know Calc 101 in order to receive a degree in business administration, I didn't know. I also didn't know why I actually enjoyed the subject, unlike everyone else in my class. Instead of loathing the course, I saw each exercise as a puzzle, like a game of Sudoku. It's because you're weird, Karla.

As I hummed my favorite pop song, I tried to decide on what to wear on Friday. Over the last couple of days, I'd gone to the mall with Darcy on the hunt for the perfect outfit. Now I was trying to choose between two little black dresses: one was long-sleeved with a plunging neckline while the other exposed more leg and had an open back. Both made me feel good and look incredibly sexy, according to Darcy—who was ecstatic that I'd already changed my mind.

"Karla!"

My heart skipped a beat when I heard that familiar voice cutting through my thoughts. I slowed down as my stepbrother Derek caught up with me, his dark hair windblown and messy.

"Hi Derek," I said with a nervous smile, feeling my cheeks heat up as he came closer. When we shared a home, I had learned to control and conceal my feelings for him. But that became more difficult ever since he left to go to university since I hardly saw him anymore, except for Christmas.

Until now.

My mouth parched as I watched him approach, and I clenched my thighs together as if that would hide the effect he had on me. Derek was on the wrestling team and the track team. The strength mixed with the cardio made his body lean but incredibly strong. He was built like a tank masked with boyish good looks. It was no wonder my sorority sisters never shut up about him.

My sorority sisters. I almost laughed thinking about it. I never considered myself the sorority girl type in the past due to all of the stereotypes. But knowing that 40% of Twin Peaks University was composed of Greek students, I wanted Derek to be proud of me—even though I didn't belong. My sisters were nice to my face but apparently talked behind my back; Darcy was the only one who had my back, filling me in while always just being there. Not even my Big Sister, Samantha, talked to me as much as Darcy did. If I was honest with myself, I didn't know why they accepted me to begin with.

I smoothed down my TBM t-shirt with its purple- and white-stitched letters as my stepbrother caught up with me.

"I heard you're coming on Friday?" he asked casually, though I caught the hopeful glitter in his ocean blue eyes.

"Wow, word gets around fast. Yeah, I was thinking about it."

"The brothers were talking about it," he explained.

"Oh." The disappointment must have been apparent on my face or in my voice, my hurt still fresh from Sunday.

Derek grabbed my arm before I could turn away, facing me to him. Heat shot through my body even as I read the concern in his pinched brows. Get a grip, Karla. He's just being brotherly.

"Everything okay?" he asked softly.

I gave Derek a weak smile. "Yup, nothing to worry about! Anyway, I heard it's BYOB? No keg?"

Derek frowned at me. "BYOB, yeah. But even so, you shouldn't be drinking." My heart skipped a beat, knowing he worried about me getting into trouble. Warmth at his protectiveness spread through me. But when the concern didn't leave his face, I rolled my eyes.

"Oh, come on Derek. I'm in college now, what did you expect?" And it's not like I hadn't already crossed the border to bar-hop in Vancouver, where I can legally drink at 19. But I'm not about to tell him that. It bothered me that he still acted like I was too young to do anything. I was a woman now, and I wished he saw that. The protectiveness I could take, but babying me? Not so much. I'll show him on Friday, my determined mind thought.

He looked down at me with an amused glint in his eyes. Self-consciously, I shifted the strap on my shoulder, not knowing what to do with Derek's gorgeous blue gaze on me. He leaned in close, and my heart stopped in my throat. Is he going to kiss me? I could feel my cheeks flush, and I closed my eyes for the moment I'd been waiting for over the past three years.

Instead of his soft lips on mine, I felt the gentle brush of his fingertips across my lips. Within seconds, my body was no longer warm from the heat emanating from his. I fluttered my eyes open again, confused, and was met with a smirk even more amused than the look he gave me a moment ago.

"You had some crumbs on your face."

Of course, I did. Shame weighed down on me. I was so stupid to think that Derek finally saw me as a woman--and that he was trying to kiss me no less! You deserve all of this, I told myself, stomping on any bit of self-worth I had left.

"I have to go to class," I muttered before running as fast as I could.

3

"You *have* to pick that one, Karla. That one's fire. You're going to have all of the Zeta brothers drooling."

Darcy was practically drooling herself, if I was being honest with myself. We both had a two-hour break between our classes, and we'd taken the opportunity to rush back to the mall for a final fitting. Darcy was dead-set on the cleavage dress. It hugged my curves and accentuated my assets.

She's right. I knew she was. It was just that I felt so self-conscious when I was so exposed—I wasn't used to it.

Tucking an ash-blonde strand of hair behind my ear, I turned around to check my backside in the mirror one more time. I was pleased with what I saw, but I wouldn't admit it. I didn't want to seem conceited.

"Are you sure?" I asked.

"Yes. Are you kidding? That other dress doesn't even compare to how hot this one is. You have to get it."

Smiling at her through the mirror, I nodded. "This is the one, then!"

I carried the mini-dress with the plunging neckline to the cashier, throwing a pair of black studded stilettos on top as an afterthought, and mentally prepared myself for what's to come.

That night, I completed my look with matte red lipstick. Darcy had helped with my makeup—smoky champagne eyeshadow to highlight the golden-brown in my hazel eyes. Doing a little twirl in the mirror, I smoothed down the dress over my curves, making sure that it didn't scrunch up anywhere. It wasn't top-notch quality, after all: my student budget couldn't afford it.

Knock, knock, knock.

"Hey, you ready? Oh my god, Karla. You look *gorge*! Let me get a look at you!" Darcy took my hand and lifted it up in the air, studying my makeup, curled hair, and outfit. "You look perfect. I'm going to have to keep a bat with me to fight the guys off you."

"Psht," I tsked her, slipping into my studded stilettos. I could already feel the cramp in my foot—these were going to make my feet ache *fast. Worth it, though.* Her compliments made me giddy. Even if only half of it was true, that's more than enough for me. I just wanted Derek's attention. *Stop it, Karla,* I scolded myself.

"Thanks, Darcy," I said, smiling warmly at my friend.

We headed downstairs and met the rest of our sisters, who were taking turns shrieking and letting out excited approvals of my outfit and each other's. *This is so not me*, I couldn't help but think. But one look at Darcy's beaming face and it felt like it sort of was me, because she'd been the only one to make sure I felt included in everything.

After a round of group photos, we Tabbies made our way to the Zee-Phi house. Darcy and I were holding onto each other to keep from toppling over; we were both in heels and most of the path from our door to theirs was cobblestoned. I twisted my ankle at least two times, but in the end, we made it there in one piece.

This is it, I thought, trying to calm myself through steady breaths. *Let's show them what you've got.*

As soon as we opened the front door, we faced a sea of people. They clustered in groups, chatting and laughing, spilling their drinks. I scanned the room for Derek. My heart raced as I wondered where he was. *He's probably off with one of the Xi Nu Chi girls.* They had a reputation for being easy, and the guys loved them for it. *But is Derek like that? Is he like his brothers?*

I shivered, trying to snap my head out of it. *He's your stepbrother, for fuck's sake.* As I tried to wedge myself through the crowd, I caught a poster on the wall: YOU ARE SAFE FROM BEING KILLED INSIDE OF THE ZETA HOUSE… FOR TONIGHT. HAVE FUN!

Well, that explained why so many Greeks weren't afraid of being eliminated from the game here.

Darcy's manicured hand led me to the kitchen where some rowdy frat boys were playing beer pong. Grabbing two red, plastic cups, she filled each of them with a healthy dose of vodka and a splash of Sprite from the half-empty bottle on the counter.

Absently, she shoved one into my chest, her eyes scanning the room. I followed her gaze, pulling up blank.

"Who are you looking for?" I finally asked, taking a sip of the strong, citrusy concoction. I scrunched my nose.

Giving me a nervous smile, she swallowed a mouthful of the cocktail. "Oh. No one. Come on, let's dance!" She grabbed my hand and tried to yank me forward.

I frowned, my heels digging into the ground, tethering us both in place. Something felt off.

"Darcy...? What aren't you telling me?"

Quickly, she gestured for us to go out onto the patio. Once outside, she closed the door and turned to me. "Okay. Promise me you won't be mad?"

My curled blonde hair slapped my cheeks as I shook my head, trying to grasp what she was saying. "Be mad? About what?"

She took a huge swig of her drink before confessing, "I didn't want to tell you this before, but I've sort of had the biggest crush on your brother for, like, ever." Darcy was still shooting glances in through the window.

"He's my *step*brother," I repeated once again through gritted teeth. "Wait, is that why you're friends with me? To get with Derek?"

Darcy gasped and blushed, shaking her head. "What? No way, Karla! You've got it all wrong. I really like you. You're super sweet!"

She sounded so fake that I almost spat my drink at her. Maybe I should have.

"Amanda told me you were the one who wanted me to join, is that true?" I demanded. When she didn't answer, I pressed, "Why would you do that if not for *him*? You barely spoke to me at the rush events... Tell me the truth!"

The pretty brunette looked stunned, her lips agape. My face twisted in disgust, and I looked off to our sorority house in the distance. Its aubergine turrets twisted up to pierce the moon. My breathing came rapidly through my nostrils.

"Well, you should be grateful," she finally managed. "At least you got a bid."

My lip curled up in a snarl and I shivered. I turned to yank open the door. Over my shoulder, I said, "You know, I thought you were better than that." I pressed my lips together before my voice could crack and entered the frat house, letting the door slam shut behind me. Setting the red Solo cup on the counter, I pushed my way past the crowd of Zeta brothers in the kitchen, huffing in annoyance at the way they whooped and hollered at their stupid game of beer pong. *I hate them. I hate all of them.*

"Karla, are you okay?" asked Samantha, her body blocking my path to the exit, concern etched on her face. Although Samantha is my Big, apparently, she said some nasty thing about me during deliberations. In fact, according to Darcy, most of our sisters had. We were likely only paired as Big and Little because I placed Samantha as my first choice. *I can't trust anyone.* I shrugged Samantha's hand off my arm and stalked to the front door.

I wanted to return my sorority pin and relinquish my status as an active sister. I wanted to drop out. Mostly, I just wanted to bury myself underneath all of my blankets and disappear in a pool of chocolate and wine. Well, mostly chocolate, I didn't really like the taste of wine. Acquired taste, Darcy kept telling me. *Well, fuck you, Darcy, and fuck your wine!*

"Leaving so soon?" my stepbrother's rich voice stopped me in my tracks. There he stood, leaning against the wall with two plastic cups full of beer. He handed one to me. "For my college-going little sis," he teased.

"*Step*," I corrected for what felt like the billionth time.

His eyes darkened, turning more serious. "We should go somewhere private and talk."

Nodding, I followed him outside. My hands shook, beer sloshing onto the grass. We walked in silence into the park separating the seven Greek houses.

"You look amazing tonight," he told me sincerely, bringing color to my cheeks.

Just tonight? A small voice in my head asked, hurt, wondering if he saw me the way his fraternity brothers did.

As if he heard my concern, he added, "Well, you always look amazing, but I love the new style you have going." Derek glanced me over as he spoke, his gaze catching on my dress a moment too long—correction: on my *cleavage*. Like he just noticed I had any.

My cheeks burned as we sat on a bench, separated from the party by a smattering of trees. I wished it was darker so he wouldn't notice my flushed face. Wishful thinking, I knew. Even in the gloom, I spotted his smirk.

I wrapped my hands around my knees, feeling the chill of the night air. His compliment still lingered in my mind, but I didn't know how to respond. It was too late to say anything now, right? That would be awkward. I pressed my lips together, hoping he would break the silence.

Even this far, the EDM music was so loud that the bench vibrated beneath me. But I heard pounding footsteps in the distance. Someone was running towards us.

"You're dead, Sawyer!" a gruff voice yelled.

"Crap, I'm his target," Derek muttered, raking a hand through his hair. He cast an irritated look over his shoulder at the guy sprinting towards us.

"Derek…," I started, not wanting this to end already. More than anything, wanting to hear what he had to say.

"Come on," he said before setting down our beers, taking my hand, and running away from the house.

I stumbled after him, but my stilettos slowed me down, sinking into the lawn with each step. Noticing my struggle, Derek paused to wrap his arms around my waist and lift me over his shoulder. He continued to sprint as if I weighed nothing.

A surge of heat tingled through me as I realized how exposed I was. I reached behind me to pull down my dress, but it was useless. I kept my hand there, hoping to cover my lacy black panties from any curious eyes, my toes thumping against his chest.

Eventually, Derek lost the Greek brother who had been tailing us, and he gently lowered me to solid ground. His fingertips grazed the tender flesh beneath my ass, sending a bolt of electric anticipation through my veins.

"Sorry," he murmured, his voice carrying hints of regret. When he looked at me, his eyes smoldered, taking my breath away. *I've never seen him look at me like that before.* Derek's jaw clenched with words unsaid, kindling a primal longing within me.

Feeling a lump form in my throat, I averted my gaze to the surrounding scenery. We stood at the edge of a secluded lake, its glossy surface mirroring the starlit sky above. Distant lights of the frat party twinkled from across the water. I was glad to be away. To be here, with Derek. I peeked at him sidelong.

"Do you bring all girls here?" I teased. Blushing, I hastily added, "Not that I'm— I just meant because it's so secluded. Like girls *other* than me."

Damn it, why am I so bad with words around him?

The corner of his full lips quirked up, recognizing my nervousness. *He's always known*, I realized, mortified.

"Look, Karla…," he started. "You're going to be invited to a lot of frat parties now and all throughout uni. I want you to be careful. You're a very sexy girl, and you need to be firm with the brothers, otherwise they'll get the wrong idea and could take advantage of you."

I was about to laugh it off, to assure him his brothers were definitely not into me, when his words registered. My body became painfully aware of how my stepbrother's voice had deepened to a husk. He took a small step towards me, one hand stroking my cheek, featherlight.

Nothing could stop the throb between my legs or the yearning of my heart. His blue eyes seared my soul, making me feel feverish and tingly. My heart thrummed a tune only reserved for Derek. When I met his gaze, the fog in my mind cleared. The way I felt wasn't one-sided. Maybe it never was. My stepbrother was simply better at concealing his feelings. I couldn't breathe.

Derek tipped his head, lowering his face to mine. "Karla..." he whispered, his voice low and full of emotion.

I couldn't take it anymore. I had to have him. Even if it was just this once. Derek's lips found mine as I closed the gap between us, wrapping my arms around his neck. His kiss was soft at first. Tender. Derek's tongue gently massaged mine, like he needed to make sure I wanted this.

Digging my hands into his hair, I parted my lips, letting my tongue collide with his. My heart galloped like it would burst, and he wrapped his strong arm around my waist, pulling me into his firm chest. *I can't believe this is happening,* I thought, my body trembling against his.

As if hearing my thoughts, Derek smiled against my lips. His tongue toyed with mine, teasing it before lightly tracing my bottom lip. encircling it with his. The kiss became more frantic. Deeper.

Slowly, Derek's other hand moved from my waist and found my breast. He squeezed me through the dress, his thumb rubbing against my nipple. I moaned into his mouth, my body heating up, yearning for more. The throbbing between my legs grew stronger as I felt his bulge grow against my stomach. Every time I pushed my hips towards his, he would press his against me in response, moving his erection against my soft flesh. A moan drew from his lips as he slipped one hand under my plunging neckline, bringing my breasts out of the confinements of the stretchy black fabric.

My kisses grew hungrier as he rolled my nipples between his fingertips. When he pinched them, I cried out his name, all strength leaving my legs. He pressed me against a tree, pushing his bulge against my mound.

Moving his lips to my ear, his breath was hot as he whispered, "I want you, Karla."

The primal, masculine tone of his voice sent chills down my spine. My stepbrother's body was so warm against mine, so strong, and it made me feel safe. A knot of desire rose in my stomach.

I couldn't stifle my gasps as Derek's mouth moved lower down my neck to my bosom. He kissed and licked the tops of my breasts, before taking a lick of my nipple, swirling his tongue around it before blowing cold air on it. My knees buckled. I gasped with need, my hips shifting against him, urging him on. When Derek couldn't take it anymore, he slipped his hands under my butt and lifted me up, my legs wrapping around his waist. The trees swayed overhead, their shadows dancing across the lake as he carried me. I didn't know where we were headed, and I didn't care. My lust-filled haze allowed me to see only him.

He lay me on the carpet of moss, the craggy ground squishing beneath us, before his mouth was on mine again. His strong hands caressed my curves, his fingertips moving up my thighs. One finger curved beneath my dress to pull my panties to the side. He teased me with his fingers, tickling the dewy flesh of my inner thighs, before I felt his fingers slip under my soaking lace thong. He groaned when he felt how slick I was for him and slid his touch right where I wanted it. I gasped, writhing against his hand.

Breaking our kiss, Derek's eyes burned into mine while he pumped a finger into me. "You have no idea how long I've wanted to do this," he murmured, his voice thick with lust.

"Me neither," I breathed, my face flushed. My stepbrother watched my pleasure like he'd never witnessed anything more exquisite.

I was so wet for him, I knew that if he wanted me right there on the grass beside the lake, he could have me. His expert fingers stroked the length of my slit, and I couldn't help but throw my head back and moan for him, my hips rocking against his fingers. Derek swallowed my moans with his mouth before trailing kisses down my chin, my neck, my breasts, and then finally lowering himself to my heat. My stepbrother placed my calves onto his shoulders, his face between my legs. Derek only hesitated for a moment, his eyes finding mine for approval before lowering his mouth. Yanking off my panties, he tossed them to the side. His tongue darted out and danced against my clit, lapping up my juices. When he slipped a finger inside me, I came undone.

"Oh god," I cried, writhing underneath him.

I didn't care how wrong it was. I didn't care about potential fallout or awkward Christmas holidays. All I knew was that I needed Derek. Right then and there. I was entirely his; I always had been. The only thing I cared about was how long I'd denied myself him; *that's* what was wrong.

As Derek's tongue stroked my pussy, his moans intensified just as mine did; he clearly enjoyed the taste of me. I could see the shape of his head through the fabric of my dress as it moved up and down, helping the long, lapping strokes of his tongue.

A knot of tension tightened in my stomach, my thighs quaking as I came against Derek's mouth. I cried out his name, my hips bucking against his lips as I came. He stayed there, licking me until my orgasm subsided, my body recovering from its shock of pleasure.

"Holy fuck," I finally managed as I was coming down. "You're incredible."

Derek straightened the hem of my dress before moving up; he tenderly kissed the top of my head. My heart melted a little bit more for him.

"And you taste incredible." His tone was thick with need.

I looked up at him with wonder. "You're not what I expected you to be," I admitted.

"No? What exactly did you expect me to be, Karla?" He nuzzled my neck as his words shot delicious tingles down my spine.

You are what you hang with, I wanted to say. But I also wanted to be more tactful. "I thought you'd be like your—"

I was interrupted by fireworks going off. My head turned towards the commotion. Gold, silver, and blue sparkles cascaded from the stars.

"Wow," I breathed, thinking that this night couldn't have ended any more perfectly, other than returning the gift Derek had given me.

"Wow is right," Derek responded through gritted teeth, glaring at his fraternity house. "Fucking idiots. I told them to keep the fireworks locked." My stepbrother jumped back onto his feet, torn between me on the grass and the hollering across the lake. He swore beneath his breath before turning to leave.

I frowned, puzzled. "What's so wrong with…," I started before remembering fireworks are illegal in Arizona. Slipping my heels off, I held them in one hand and rushed to meet his quick pace. "Derek, hold up!" I said, not wanting the night to end so soon.

He paused for a moment, glancing back at me. "I'm sorry, Karla. I really am. The lease is under my name, so I have to get back there ASAP before they do anything else stupid… Or before the cops show up." Derek stroked my cheek tenderly with the back of his hand, looking as regretful as ever. "This isn't over," he promised before turning and sprinting as fast as he could back to the frat house.

I stood watching him and the distant fraternity house, dumbfounded. *How did Derek get away with signing the lease on a multi-million-dollar house?*

His figure shrunk in the distance before disappearing in the shadows, my questions trailing after him. Fireworks continued to pop off overhead, sprinkling over the lake.

Thoughts raced through my mind. Derek kept his feelings from me—what else was he hiding? Exhaling sharply, I decided we were due for another heart-to-heart. This time, I was determined to keep it hands off.

4

On Saturdays, Darcy's Little Sister Mona liked to prepare a pancake breakfast for the sisters. Only thirty of us lived in the house, but the weekend madness would make you think there were more than one hundred. Normally this irked me, but I was thankful for the chaos on this particular hungover morning.

After Derek left, I'd returned to my room and proceeded to finish the booze I had stowed while browsing through his TikTok videos. Darcy had sent me several text messages throughout the night, wanting me to come back to the party, wanting to talk. I deleted every single one.

But I knew I'd likely run into her this morning. Skipping Mona's pancake breakfast was unheard of. She went all out, always presenting it with bowls of chocolate chips, strawberries, blueberries, and whipped cream. Exactly what we needed after a night of heavy drinking—or after any night, period.

Groggily, I slipped on my sweatpants and trotted downstairs. Excited chatter floated through the hall, the girls talking about last night's hookups, any embarrassing moments, who was off limits, and common heartthrobs. Derek's name came up more than once.

Jealousy bubbled inside me as I loaded my plate with pancakes, a healthy serving of strawberries, and a small mountain of whipped cream. I headed back to my room before I could snap at my sisters to not talk about Derek that way, but I stopped when someone grabbed my forearm.

"Can we talk?" It was Darcy, her tone somber.

I shrugged. "Depends, are you going to try to use me some more?"

"Karla, I'm serious. I don't want to lose you as a friend," she pleaded.

My anger flared, remembering why we were fighting to begin with, remembering that she had a crush on Derek. *Mine.* It was wrong, but I knew it in my body, in my bones: Derek was mine. As much as Darcy had been a good friend these past few months, if I was going to pick between my sisters and Derek… Well, there was no competition.

Shaking her arm off me, I continued upstairs. "Were we ever really friends to begin with?" I retorted, wanting to hit her where it hurt. A small part of me also wanted her to back off of Derek, but I knew if she did then I'd wonder if Derek chose me just because there was no other competition or because he actually liked me.

"Karla," Darcy whined. "Please!"

Glaring at her over my shoulder, I burned the bridge. "You were never a good sister, Darcy. And you have terrible eyebrows."

5

It had been four days since the lake with Derek. My heart ached, wondering if he thought what we did was a mistake, praying that he didn't think it was. Darcy had avoided me in the halls every time I passed her. *Good riddance,* I kept telling myself, convinced that she was mainly upset that I wouldn't put a good word in for her with my stepbrother.

I'm so stupid, I thought with a pang. With every passing moment, I was more and more convinced that I needed to drop out of Tau Beta Mu. Greek life just wasn't for me. I should have known from the start.

In my mind, it was settled: I would relinquish my rights as an active sister. *I'll do it after class.* I chewed on the rubber end of my pencil as I eyed the clock on the wall. It was 3:19 PM; my Organizational Behavior class would end any second.

The moment the hands ticked to 3:20, I shot up out of my seat, shoved my pencil and notebook into my backpack, and rushed out the door.

"Hey, Karla!" called an unfamiliar male voice once I exited the lecture hall.

Confused, I glanced over my shoulder, spotting a golden-haired prep sauntering in my direction. He was dressed in a tailored polo shirt and corduroy pants that looked more expensive than my entire wardrobe. When my eyes met his, he flashed a dazzling smile. One that likely melted panties.

"Yes?" I reschooled my puzzled expression into a smile.

"You're Derek's sister, right?" It didn't really sound like a question. I parted my lips to correct him but the way he looked at me said he wasn't interested in semantics, so I nodded. He grinned. "Great. Come with me."

I followed the stranger, curiosity getting the best of me. He stalked down the hall and exited through the emergency exit; I scrambled to keep up.

"Um, why?" I asked. "Why do I need to follow you, I mean?"

"You don't have any more classes today, do you?" He flicked a look down at me.

I shook my head.

"Well, don't worry about it, then." He shot me a wry smile. "Hey, you're kinda cute," he added, pinching the top of my exposed cleavage.

Mortified, I distanced myself from him and folded my arms over my chest. "Sorry, but what the fuck was that for?"

I hadn't meant to sound so heated, but I couldn't help it. It seriously pissed me off when *fuckboys* thought they had free reign of my body because of their status, money, or looks. *Piece of shit.*

"I was just messing around," he chortled, but his eyes shamelessly roamed over my curves. Assessing the goods.

Suddenly, I felt a pair of strong arms lift me up, slinging me over their shoulder like a ragdoll. Poking my head up, I spotted three unfamiliar but equally preppy guys briskly walking away from campus, towards the Greek houses. One wore a blazer. When the flap of his jacket flipped open, I spotted the letters emblazoned on his navy-blue shirt: Mu Beta Alpha. The most prestigious fraternity on campus. If Xi Nu Chi was the Queen of sororities at Twin Peaks Uni, then Mu Beta Alpha was the King.

Silly, naïve, Karla, I internally yelled at myself. "What do you want with me?" I asked, tampering the wail in my voice.

Golden fratboy shot a sly grin my way. "Payback."

Throughout the next few hours, I learned that Derek had rushed for all of the fraternities and Mu Beta Alpha had extended a bid to him. Derek had accepted Zeta Phi Pi's bid instead. Derek was the first person to turn down the organization, thoroughly pissing off the brotherhood. They had waited to get their revenge for a while, but Derek had been untouchable. Until they learned about me.

Squirming on the cream leather sofa, I said with a sigh, "Look, I have an assignment to get to. I really don't have time for this."

Tanned golden boy looked at me and snorted. Behind him hung a giant portrait of a seemingly fart-sniffing man. Probably a founder of the group.

When it was clear he wouldn't respond, I tried to stand. Strange hands pushed my shoulders back down.

"You'll wait here until your brother shows up," Golden Fratboy said. "We know he wouldn't resist coming for you."

"What do you mean?" I asked, hoping I kept most of the panic out of my voice. A few of the brothers snickered, sharing knowing glances. I hid my trembling hands under my butt, glancing between them.

Just then, my phone vibrated. I pulled it out of my pocket. There were several unread messages from Darcy, and I swiped right to remove them from my notifications list. The last one caught my attention.

FOUR PEOPLE LEFT ALIVE, Callie had posted on the public Facebook page for the game.

The game's still going on? I hmphed, scanning the list of names; my lips formed an 'o' when I realized I'm a finalist. I tugged my sleeve over the Kandi bracelet. If I was going to be 'killed', I didn't want it to be while I was held hostage in Mu

Beta Alpha's living room. There was a knock on their front door.

"That must be your brother now," Goldenboy said, his mouth twisting up. He left the room to investigate.

Glancing around, I realized that I was now alone. *This is my chance.* In the distance, I could hear my blond captor murmuring with whoever was at the door. Slowly, I got to my feet and tiptoed to the wall, craning my neck around the bend to see if I could spot an exit.

A sharp, scraping sound caught my attention, and I whipped my head around. Derek stared at me from the opposite side of the window, inching up the pane with both hands. He beckoned me with a nod. I double-glanced over my shoulder at the back of my captor's head before rushing across the room toward my stepbrother. I helped open up the window the rest of the way. Before I could say anything, Derek looped an arm around my waist and pulled me out the window, against his chest. Once on solid footing, he interlaced his fingers with mine, and then we made a run for it.

We slowed once the lake came into view. My heart immediately leapt at the sight of it, memories of what happened the other night flooding my vision. I peeked sidelong at Derek; from his hooded gaze, I knew he was thinking about the same thing.

His fingers slipped out of mine, and suddenly I felt both strange and empty. Strange because it hadn't occurred to me that we'd been holding hands the entire time—it felt so natural that it melded in with everything else that was going on. Empty because now that I'd lost what I didn't know I had, I desperately wanted it back.

I picked up my pace, swinging my arms close to his to 'accidentally' brush our fingers together to see if he would notice. He didn't.

Derek's attention was fixed on the trail to the lake, his eyes scanning like he was on a mission.

Daring to break the silence, I asked, "Uh, Derek, what happened back there?"

Setting his jaw, he shook his head. "Nothing for you to worry about."

"It is though, isn't it? Since they just kidnapped me and all."

Derek narrowed his eyes, a faraway look entering his face.

I pressed softly, "Are they really that mad over something that happened years ago?"

After a moment, he gave me a tight smile. "Something like that. It's…complicated. I'll deal with it. Don't worry about it, baby."

My heart flip-flopped at the nickname, and I couldn't help the warmth spreading through my chest. Clearing my throat, I asked, "So… Where are we going?"

Grinning widely, he said, "It's a surprise. I just need to spot the right…" He cut himself off and knelt beside a rose bush, shifting dried leaves before letting out a triumphant grunt. "Here," he announced, tugging out a covered wicker basket from the confinements of Mother Nature.

I arched an eyebrow, my curiosity piqued. "What's in there?"

Derek winked playfully at me. "You'll see."

We hiked for a few more minutes until we arrived at a clearing—the same one he took me to on Friday night. The sun was peaking over the horizon, casting a warm glow over the water. The wind picked up, carrying the faint scent of jasmine. I took a deep breath, feeling a sense of calm wash over me.

Derek spread out a blanket and motioned for me to sit. He opened the basket, revealing a spread of fresh fruit, cheese, crackers, and a bottle of champagne.

My breath caught in my throat. "Did you plan all of this?"

He grinned, pouring us each a glass of champagne. "I may have had some help."

I took a sip of the bubbly liquid, feeling it tickle my nose. My heart fluttered with the realization that *Derek*, of all people, had gone through this much trouble—for me. "This is amazing. Thank you," I said softly.

Sheepishly, he answered, "I felt bad for how we left things off on Friday, so I thought we could hang out."

"Hang out?" *Is that what you call romantic, lakeside picnics?* I wanted to tease, but I didn't want to spoil the moment.

The atmosphere around us was charged with a kind of electricity that I couldn't ignore. I could feel my heart pounding in my chest, as if it was trying to beat its way out. The way Derek was looking at me, his eyes dark and intense, only made my heart race faster.

"I really care about you, Karla," he murmured, his fingertips tracing circles on the back of my hand.

"I care about you, too," I said, my voice barely above a whisper.

Derek leaned in and brushed his lips against mine, a gentle and sweet kiss. My heart fluttered at the contact, and I pulled him in for another. His hands cupped my face as he deepened the kiss. I moaned softly, feeling every inch of my body come alive under his touch.

He broke the kiss and looked into my eyes, a serious expression on his face. "You know, this is dangerous, right?" Derek asked, his voice low and urgent.

"Maybe I like living on the edge, sir," I teased, shrugging with one shoulder.

"Sir?" He arched an eyebrow, baring his teeth in a wolfish grin.

I giggled. "I was just acting."

"I know," he responded huskily. "Do it again."

"Um, I don't know what to say... sir?"

His grin widened. "You're so fucking cute, you know that?"

With a pounding heart, I gave him a small smile. "No?" *How do I even respond to that?*

Derek chuckled and leaned in to kiss me again, his fingers tangling in my hair. The kiss was different now, charged with a new level of intensity. His tongue teased mine, sending shivers down my spine. I pressed myself closer to him, my hands roaming over his chest.

He pulled back, his forehead resting against mine. "We need to stop," he said, his breath hot on my lips. "At least for now."

I pouted, disappointment weighing on me. "Why?"

"Because I don't want to rush things," he said, his sapphire eyes locked with mine.

"This is what I want," I assured him, bringing his hands back to my body. "Believe me. This is what I've been waiting for."

"I just don't want to drag you into something you can't get yourself out of…" he started, his pained voice trailing off.

"What do you mean?" Frowning, I slid off of his lap and sat beside him.

"Karla," my stepbrother sighed sadly. "What do you think your mom or my dad would do if they found out? What would my fraternity do? Or your sorority?"

"We can keep it our secret," I said. *Where is he going with this?* "You can't possibly be asking that we stop already? Unless you'd given these zero thoughts, how could you possibly do that to me?" My body fought back tears as I spoke, and I distracted myself by taking a healthy swig of champagne, emptying the flute.

Derek sighed heavily, pinching the bridge of his nose. "I'm not saying we have to stop, Karla," he said, his voice heavy with emotion. "But we need to be careful. We can't let anyone find out about us. It could ruin everything."

I stared at him in disbelief. How could he think that our love was something that could be ruined? It wasn't as if we were blood-related. *But he never said he loved me, only words he's probably told a hundred different girls before.*

My hands trembled and I withdrew them from his. I tugged a daisy out of the dirt, plucking each of its petals as my stepbrother struggled with his words. Understanding, yet not wanting to understand. *He loves me, he loves me not.*

When the silence stretched, I couldn't keep the bitterness from my voice. "So that's it, huh? You've had everyone else at uni and wanted to see if you could screw around with your stepsister, too?" I barked out a laugh, letting the champagne flute roll down the grass and drop into the lake. "Well, congratulations."

Blinking rapidly, I hadn't even noticed that I'd started crying. Derek was talking, but I wasn't processing anything he was saying. My thoughts swirled angrily. Derek betrayed me, just like everyone else. I shook his hands off me and stood up, not wanting to spend another second with him. Not wanting to spend another second here. Within one quick week, I'd gone from thinking I'd finally found a place I belonged to absolutely hating it at Twin Peaks University. My feet shot forward, away from him and the picnic I'd foolishly thought was so special.

"Karla!" He yelled after me. I didn't slow down.

I stumbled back into the TBM sorority house and slammed the door behind me. I had to get away from Derek, from everything, before I lost it completely. My heart was shattered into a million pieces, and I couldn't bear the thought of spending another second with him. I dragged myself up to my room and collapsed onto my bed.

My pillow was soaked with tears, and I buried my face in it, letting out a ragged sob. How could I have been so dumb? How could I have fallen for my stepbrother? And how could he have led me on like that, only to crush me so heartlessly?

My mind raced with a million different thoughts, and I couldn't focus on anything else. I didn't know how long I lay there, lost in my own thoughts, shrill laughter from the room next door drew jerked my attention. From Darcy's room. Squeezing my eyes shut, I covered my face with a pillow, but girly voices floated through to my room.

"Are you sure he's there?" asked one of the girls—Mona, I think.

Darcy replied, "Yup! Max said he'd be hanging out by the lake for a while. You don't think I'm dressed too slutty for a casual evening walk, do you?"

Both girls burst into a fit of giggles. Then Darcy's door slammed shut. My skin prickled with a potpourri of emotions. *Go ahead and find him,* I thought bitterly, digging my nails into the palms of my hands.

6

I swirled the coffee around in my mug as I stared at the homework I'd spread across the large table, big enough to seat six people. The rest of the coffeeshop was packed with people. I was beyond caring. If someone wanted to have somewhere to sit badly enough, they could ask. Nicely.

My gaze floated around the small campus coffee shop, wishing for a certain face to appear but never seeing it.

I checked my phone for notifications. Found none. No surprise there. All of my friends were sisters, and none of them had reached out to me. Not since Darcy had gone around spewing bullshit about how I had 'betrayed' a sister—an offense that could result in expulsion from the sisterhood. That's the cost of not participating in spouting petty rumors and not caring enough to clear the gossip about me. *So, expel me. I was going to drop out after class yesterday anyway.* The emotional drain stopped me.

But if Amanda, the president of TBM, wanted to kick me out, then that would make it a lot easier for me.

My phone vibrated, and I snatched it off the table. Disappointment filled me when I read that it was just a mass message: *Only three people left in this Spring semester's game of Killer! Trust no one.*

Who the fuck cares? I thought, then my attention snagged on another email from Callie: "Karla, Your target dropped out of the game. Your new target is… DARCY SNAKE. Good luck, have fun!"

Typical. I rolled my eyes, the words quivering in my trembling hand. Swiping through my contacts, I dialed the only person I could think to. Mom picked up after three rings.

"Hel-lo?" she answered, her voice choking.

"Mom? Is everything okay?"

"Oh, honey," she let out a silent sob.

Concern filled me. "I'm coming home," I said firmly, gathering my papers and shoving them in my backpack, not caring if they all became crumpled in there.

"No!" My mom practically yelled it, and it made me stop half-paper-shove. "I mean… There's just— It's just-"

"Mom, just tell me what's going on. Please!"

"We were waiting for the right time to tell you. It's no surprise that Roderick and I fight all the time. We decided about a year ago that we weren't right for each other but wanted to make sure that you were sent off to college before we did… We didn't want anything interfering with your education—or Derek's."

"Wait. You're splitting up?" I almost knocked over the mug of cold coffee.

"I'm staying with your Grandma Gemma right now, until we get all of the paperwork sorted."

But Grandma Gemma's all the way in Maine… I decided to not scold her for abandoning me in Arizona while she was on the other side of the country. Instead, I softly asked, "Can I do anything to help?"

Apparently, I couldn't. We said our goodbyes and hung up with the promise that I'd fly over to Maine after finals.

Stunned, I slung my backpack over my shoulder and kept my head down as I left the coffee shop. I didn't know who witnessed my phone call, and I didn't want to know.

A strong arm gripped my bicep, and I almost elbowed the intruder in response after what happened in class on Tuesday. My lips parted when my eyes locked with the sapphire-eyed intruder's: Derek's.

"We need to talk," he said, dragging me along with him.

"About what? How you royally broke my heart?" I snapped, not caring who was around us or was listening.

"Not here." My stepbrother's voice was hushed as he led me to the alley behind the coffee shop.

Tears swelled in my eyes as we entered the dark alley and Derek rounded on me, but I blinked them back and glared at him.

"Why?" I breathed, wanting to know what he had to say.

"I can't explain it without ruining everything." Derek groaned, running his hands through his dark brown hair.

"What's there to ruin?" I laughed dryly. "You had your fun with me, now you can go back to playing your stupid game and I can go—"

"Karla," my stepbrother actually pleaded with me. "Don't."

"Don't what? Don't care about you?" My voice cracked. "The only reason I even let you—"

"Shh," he said, putting a finger to my lips as he glanced around.

Within seconds, I heard it: *clack, clack, clack.* Someone on the hunt. Glancing past the dumpsters, I saw Darcy's long hair swish as she rushed towards us.

"I knew it!" she shrieked, pointing her phone at us with one hand and holding a Sharpie in the other.

I stepped back, trying to put as much distance between myself and Darcy as possible. Derek stepped forward, shielding me from her with his body.

"Leave her alone, Darcy," he growled, his voice low and menacing.

Darcy cackled, twirling the Sharpie around in her hand. "You're not the boss of me, Derek. And now, thanks to this picture, I have the proof I need to get what I want."

My heart sank as I saw the photo she was talking about. It was a picture of me and Derek at the lake. Yesterday. Derek had his arm around my waist and our faces were dangerously close to a kiss. My face burned.

"Give me that," Derek snarled, reaching for her phone. Darcy danced out of his reach, holding the phone high above her head.

"Uh uh. You're not getting it that easy," Darcy taunted, sticking her tongue out at Derek.

"What do you want?" I asked, staring at her in confusion.

But my ex-friend's eyes glittered as she stared up at my stepbrother, her lips curving into a wicked grin. Multi-colored Kandi bracelets covered her forearm. *If she wins, she gets him to herself for one night,* I thought, remembering the prize.

Darcy took a slow step towards Derek, uncapping the Sharpie. Without thinking, I lunged towards her and swatted the permanent marker out of her hand.

"You're disgusting," she spat at me. "Fooling around with your own brother. I can't believe I ever called you my sister."

I rushed for the pen and Darcy followed suit, but I grabbed a fistful of her long hair and yanked her away from the pen.

"Well, I can't believe I ever called you my friend," I seethed, my ears roaring. "You're nothing but a manipulative, backstabbing bitch." Her face twisted into an ugly grimace; it surprised me that I never realized how fake she was before this whole ordeal.

"Skank!" she cried out, her hand going up to touch her scalp, finding her hair intact.

I took her moment of confusion to charge her, pen outstretched, and I drew a huge X across her right cheek.

Startled, she pressed her hand against it as if I'd slapped her.

"Now you look as ugly as you are on the inside," I said. "By the way, you were my target, and you're dead."

Without glancing back, I left the alley. I didn't take her Kandi. I already had Derek at my side.

7

We ended up in one of the library's private study rooms. Derek didn't know about our parents; I knew he didn't from the way he was acting, and I wanted to keep it that way until I knew how he truly felt. Was he playing with me or was there really more to it?

He booked the most secluded study room in the entire library, one that was separated by a storage room *and* a janitorial room, unlike all the other rooms that were mostly cramped together.

Once inside, Derek took a seat and I made sure to choose one across from him, not daring sit next to him. I couldn't trust myself to be that close to him.

"I hate how things ended the other day," he started.

"You mean with you telling me it wasn't going to work out?" I couldn't help it. I'd meant to bite my tongue, but the emotions were still so raw I just needed to lash out at him.

"That's *not* what it was about. You didn't even let me finish before you stormed off."

Exasperated, Derek raked his fingers through his dark hair. "Look, I've never had this problem before."

"So I'm a problem now?"

"*No*. Can you stop twisting everything I saw for two seconds? What I'm trying to tell you is that... Fuck, Karla, I've never had feelings for anyone like this before, okay? Normally girls I hook up with are just that: a hook-up. But you're so much more than that, so I wanted to make sure I did everything right. I didn't expect it to backfire so hard."

My heart was pounding even as I stayed silent, though I was sure he could hear it. My phone buzzed in my pocket. I silenced it without looking at who it was. When he didn't continue, I prodded hopefully, "So... you're saying you have feelings for me?"

"Yes, genius."

Butterflies ran amuck in my belly. 'Genius' was a familiar taunt between us—one that started when my mom and I moved into his house. I couldn't help but grin, the sullen mood draining out of me.

"What does this mean?" I asked. "To you, I mean."

I dared steal a glance at my stepbrother—my former stepbrother, I mean. He stared down at his clenched fist, flexing it out on the table before raising his eyes to mine. I knew whatever he had to say was tearing him up inside, and my heart dropped at the sight of it. *He's going to say it won't work out.* The fear crept through my bones.

But once again, Derek surprised me. "I'm dropping out of the brotherhood."

My mouth fell open; he *loved* his fraternity.

"It's the only way," he explained, but I had the feeling he was trying to explain it to himself. "While it's not against the rules, I know what kind of strain it'd have on the frat if they found out one of their brothers was dating his stepsister."

"They don't have to find out," I rushed, wanting to ease his pain. "I'm thinking of dropping the sorority and, hell, even out of university. No one would know who I am."

Derek just shook his head sadly. "It wouldn't matter. Your sisters still know who you are, and word would spread *fast*."

My phone began vibrating again. Amanda's face flashed on the screen. Calls from the president were unheard of. I frowned but silenced my phone anyway. This time, the call was followed with a text: "Urgent meeting—come to the house".

"You should go," Derek said.

"No, it doesn't matter." *I'm so done with the Tabbies.*

My ex-stepbrother looked at me like he wasn't going to take no for an answer. "It *does* matter. Don't drop out, okay? I'll figure out a way around this, I just wanted you to know that I'm trying my best to make this work. That I do care, in spite of what you think. Remember that."

He looked so distraught, leaning into the table like he was going to tear it apart at any second. My lips parted, something inside me urging me to tell him that it will be okay. That we aren't step-siblings. But that isn't my story to tell.

I nodded at him, gathering my things. If I was being honest with myself, I needed time to process things, too.

When I walked into the Tau Beta Mu living room, the only person in sight was Amanda.

"Where is everyone?" I asked, glancing around.

"Off to prepare the Sister Relinquishing ceremony," she responded, her voice carrying a sad lilt.

I nodded, understanding. It wasn't Amanda's fault the other sisters didn't like me, even though they hadn't even given me a chance.

"Have a seat," she said, gesturing to the empty seat opposite her.

"We don't need to drag this out," I said, feeling defeated. "I can pack my things and leave now."

The pretty redhead furrowed her brows. "Where are you going?"

"I'd just rather not prolong the process." I stood to head to my room, but Amanda was quicker and gently gripped my arm.

"Karla." Her green eyes widened. "It's *Darcy* we're kicking out, not you!"

Gaping at her, I responded dumbly, "But Darcy's been a sister for three years!"

"And she wasn't being very sisterly. Samantha found out that Darcy had been talking about you behind your back. That she blew some of the Zee-Phi pledges in exchange for having them follow you. I wish I'd known about the bullying sooner." Her gemstone eyes glistened. *Amanda could even make crying look pretty*, my mind jabbed, but I was overcome with joy—and confusion. They wanted me. They *liked* me. Darcy had lied about everything from the start. I was almost tempted to leap up and do a dance.

"She had me followed? What did she say?" I asked.

"It doesn't matter. None of that matters," Amanda responded sternly. "What matters is that this taught us a very valuable lesson about sisterhood. From now on, we'll be hosting more sisterhood events so you can get to know us and us you."

Tears pricked at the corners of my eyes. All this time I'd felt unwanted here, and all I had to do was go and talk to one of my sisters. Seeing my surfacing emotions, my sorority's president pulled me in to a hug.

"Oh, sweetie, I'm so sorry." She stroked my hair gently. "We all know, by the way," she said softly. When I didn't pretend I knew what she was talking about, Amanda proceeded, "About you... and Derek. Darcy made sure to tell everyone. But I just want you to know that we support you fully. You can't control who your heart loves, and we're rooting for you."

I broke out into a wobbly smile, a tear spilling over. I laughed through a sob. "It feels incredible to hear you say that, Amanda. Honestly. Thank you so much."

She responded with a warm smile. "What are sisters for?"

"If it makes any difference, he's not my stepbrother anymore. Our parents just broke up."

But from Amanda's reaction, it didn't make a damn difference at all. She loved me all the same.

And for the first time, I was certain my sisters did, too.

8

You awake?

It was Derek. I stared at the text, my finger hovering over the digital keyboard. After my meeting with Amanda, I'd wanted to rush over to him, to tell him the good news about how supportive my girls were and how our parents weren't together anyway. I stopped myself, though.

As incredible, funny, smart, and sexy Derek was, I didn't want to jump into a relationship that he wasn't willing to fight for. I didn't need a man, or anyone, to make me happy, and I wasn't interested in heartache, if that's what he was planning on dishing. So I'd waited to hear back from him to make sure he was as into me as I was him.

I swiped in my response.

Yeah. Wanna talk? I asked, then flung my phone under my pillow when I saw the three flashing dots. I could feel my nerves all the way through my fingertips, and I chewed my bottom lip as I waited.

The vibration came a moment later.

Come over.

I froze, excited, anxious, and suddenly feeling incredibly shy. It made sense for me to go to his house, because he had the bedroom in the basement beside the huge dance floor. It was a disadvantage when they threw parties, but an advantage literally every other day of the year. His room was the most private in the fraternity mansion.

I didn't bother changing out of my sleepwear. I tied a plush robe around me, slipped into flats, and darted across the park to his frat house. He was waiting at the door when I arrived; after a quick embrace, he hurried me downstairs. We moved quietly, not wanting to wake anyone or draw attention.

Once in his room, I casually leaned against his wall in an attempt to look cool and collected.

"So, what's up?" I asked breathlessly.

My robe slipped open, momentarily revealing my silky purple nightdress. Derek caught a glimpse, his gaze darkening at the sight. Blushing, I reinforced the knot at my waist, hoping to hide my embarrassment. I looked around his room, feeling a jolt of recognition. The same framed posters for The

Beatles and Nick Cave & the Black Seeds lined his wall. The same navy-blue bedspread covered his bed. It almost felt as if we were back home. Nibbling the insides of my cheeks, I took a seat at the edge of Derek's bed as I waited expectantly for him to start the conversation. Derek noticed my discomfort and moved closer to sit beside me, his hand cupping my cheek.

"Karla, I wanted to talk about us," he said slowly.

My heart thundered as my eyes locked onto his. I couldn't deny the attraction between us, and I wasn't sure I wanted to.

"I know things have been complicated, with our parents and everything," he continued, his voice low and husky. "But I can't stop thinking about you. And I don't want to. There's something I want to talk to you about."

He reached out, taking my hand in his. The touch sent shivers down my spine, but I wanted to hear what he had to say before I let him touch me, so I shifted away from him, as empty as it made me feel.

Hurt flashed across his face, but he nodded in understanding.

"Well, two points, actually, and they don't influence each other."

"Go on," I urged him.

"The Zee-Phis know."

"About us?"

Derek nodded. "That photo Darcy had on her phone was one of many. Most were shared on Snapchat. Videos, too."

"Oh." My face burned with embarrassment and shame. *I can't believe everyone knows about us. That people were eavesdropping on what we did.*

"But..." Derek hesitated, his eyes searching mine. "They don't care. At least, not the ones who matter. Amanda and a few others came up to me after today's chapter meeting and said the TMB girls support us, too. They even apologized for not being more welcoming to you before."

My heart swelled with gratitude and love for my sorority sisters. "That's amazing. I had a talk with Amanda earlier today, and she said the same thing."

Derek smiled, relief evident on his face. "That's great to hear. And the second point…" He trailed off, his thumb rubbing circles on the back of my hand. "Karla, I know we've been tiptoeing around this, but I need to say it. I'm in love with you."

My breath caught in my throat as his words hit me like a bullet.

"Nothing can change how I feel about you. Not my dad. Not the frat. Nothing. And I don't ever want you to feel like you're a secret. Hell, I want to show you off to the world. That was my second point."

I bit my lip as my heart pounded in my chest. "So, you're saying...?"

"I want to be with you, Karla. I want you to be mine."

I leaned in and kissed him hard, my hands fisting his shirt. I couldn't believe how happy I was in that moment. I'd waited so long for him to say those words. Fantasized about it while I lulled myself to sleep so many times. To hear him tell me that he loved me and that he wanted me. And now, my dream had come true.

"I love you too," I whispered, my lips still pressed against his. "More than anything."

He groaned and pulled me closer, our mouths meeting in a kiss that was both passionate and filled with promise. His tongue tangled with mine, and I felt as if I was drowning in a sea of desire. I knew that I wanted him, all of him, and that I would do anything to keep him by my side.

"I was hoping you'd say that," he murmured against my lips. His hand came up to stroke my hair and cheek as he kissed me, his other hand interlocking with mine and holding it firmly above my head.

"What's this?" I asked, glancing up at my pinned arm.

Flashing me a brilliant smile, he responded with a wink, "I just want to make sure I've got you where I want you."

The implication was clear, and I felt a hot flush spread through my body. Derek was always full of surprises, and I didn't know what to expect from him. But I trusted him, and I knew that he would never hurt me.

I leaned into him, breathing in his warm, musky scent. His hands roamed over my body, sending shivers down my spine. I moaned softly, feeling a rush of pleasure that was almost overwhelming. Derek's lips trailed down my neck, leaving a fiery path in its wake. His hands caressed my breasts through the thin fabric of my nightgown, making me gasp. I arched my back, pressing myself against him. He groaned, his fingers digging into my skin as he pulled me closer.

"Now, let's see this outfit you've been hiding from me since you got here," he whispered huskily as he held my arms above my head, undoing the knot at my waist. My robe fell open, and he growled a satisfied 'mmm' from deep within his throat.

Licking his lips, Derek brought his head down to my neck and left a soft trail of kisses from my jawline to my collarbone before moving back up and sucking gently, marking his territory on my neck. A shiver ran through me as he kissed the tender flesh, and I tilted my head to the side to give him better access.

His free hand continued its journey down my body, ending underneath my panties. I let out a soft gasp when he found me wet and eager. With his thumb on my clit, he moved his middle finger to my entrance and slipped it inside.

Derek's eyes clouded with midnight blue desire. "So fucking wet," he murmured against my lips. His soft touch was driving me mad, and I arched my back again, moaning at the friction. His fingers slipped in and out of me, teasing and caressing my insides. I was so close, so tight.

"Derek, I'm so close," I whimpered, my breath hitching in my throat.

"Come for me, gorgeous. Let me feel you close around my fingers." His words sent me over the edge, and I moaned, my eyes fluttering closed as my breathing quickened. Derek held me close as my orgasm crashed over me, my back arching sharply as I shuddered in his arms.

I fell back against the bed, the white sheets cool against my skin. Derek followed and kissed me deeply, his tongue exploring my mouth. I moaned softly as he slid upwards, bringing his body over mine.

"I need you," he whispered hoarsely, his breath hot against my ear.

"So, take me," I said, thrusting my hips up to feel his hard manhood through the fabric of his pajamas. I slipped my hands down to tug them off, but he shook his head.

"Keep your hands above your head, gorgeous," he breathed.

I grinned, my eyes on his, then put my hands back up above my head as he had instructed.

"Good girl," he murmured approvingly.

I felt the cool air tickle my bare skin as Derek removed my robe completely, his eyes roving over my body. He traced his finger along the inside of my knee and up my thighs, then hooked his fingers under my panties and slowly slid them off of me.

I bit my lip, feeling exposed, bared to his hungry gaze. Derek looked at me like I was the most precious thing in the world, his midnight blue eyes glowing in the half-light of the room. Grinning, Derek slowly stripped out of his clothes. I bit back a moan as I ogled his cut physique, a body proving his years of hard workouts.

Then, he moved towards me and slipped my robe off of me, hanging it on the back of his desk chair. When I moved to take off my babydoll, he tsked, his lip quirking in amusement. I grinned and put my hands back above my head. Derek's eyes darkened as his gaze slid over my body.

Kneeling between my thighs, Derek brought his face down to mine, his lips brushing against mine in featherlight kisses. When he pulled away, I let out a moan of protest.

"I love you," he said softly, his tone almost reverent as his eyes locked with mine.

"I love you too," I whispered back.

I felt his hardness press against my entrance, and I arched my back, yearning for him to be inside me. Derek slid in slowly, barely an inch, and I squirmed underneath him, wanting more of him inside me. let out a soft moan of contentment, feeling myself stretched to accommodate him.

With a smirk, he pulled himself out of me. "Patience, Karla."

I ached for him. It took everything in me to hold still and maintain eye contact. The longer I did, the more he throbbed against my opening. I trembled underneath him, my pleasure trickling down the inside of my thigh.

Derek's gaze hooded as he continued to watch me, my every reaction visible to him. I moaned, I gasped, and I writhed underneath him, my body yearning for his.

"Please, Derek," I begged.

"Please what?"

He was torturing me, and I loved every second of it. "I want you, Derek. All of you."

"All of me?" he asked, a mischievous grin playing on his lips.

"All of you." I repeated, my voice rising in pitch.

I arched my back towards him, keeping my hands up over my head, though I desperately wanted to wrap my arms around his neck. Derek grabbed my thighs and spread them; His pace was excruciatingly slow. Instinctively, I wrapped my legs around his waist.

Derek's mouth covered mine as he eased himself into me, and I moaned into it from the pleasure of how completely and perfectly he filled me. Every inch of my skin prickled with anticipation.

As he filled me, he moved leisurely, pausing every time I'd breathe sharply in an attempt to adjust to his massive girth. It was hot watching him, because I could tell he was holding himself back. Once I'd finally adjusted, he began picking up his pace as he moved in and out of me. My hands came down to dig into his hair, and he quickly pinned them back up above my head. He used his free hand as leverage as he built up speed, and I could feel my heart begin to race for what was to come next.

Derek's eyes burned into mine, carefully watching my expression as he thrust himself deeper inside me. I cried out in pleasure and his hand tightened around my wrists, his hips rhythmically moving in and out of me faster and faster. Derek groaned into my mouth, and my heart flipped at the sound of his pleasure. The louder I moaned, the harder he drove into me. Craving more of him, I wriggled my wrists free and grabbed his ass, trying to pull him further into me. A dark chuckle escaped his lips.

"Are you sure you want to play it rough?" he teased, his voice a soft rumble with a hint of danger.

Squirming underneath him, I felt bold and said, "Yeah, it's my turn to take charge."

"Take charge then," he ordered, his hands finding their way back to my wrists, pinning me down.

As I wiggled under him, trying to break free again, my heart thumped even harder with desire. He drove me wild with the smug, amused look he shot me. "That's what I thought."

I squirmed underneath him, feeling my release build. "Derek," I moaned desperately.

He let out a dark laugh, letting go of my wrists and pulling out of me. His fingers roughly found their way to my waist and flipped me over. Looping his muscular arm under my hips, he tugged my ass up into the air, exposing me to him and making me feel incredibly vulnerable.

With his fingers digging into my flesh, he held me still as he thrust himself into me. I cried out in pleasure. This angle was different, even deeper than before. He began to move faster, and I could hear him breathing harder as he increased his pace.

Derek's thrusts became more urgent as he picked up speed; his cock was throbbing inside of me so much that I had to work to accommodate the extra girth. With each primal grunt he gave, I matched it was an equally passionate moan. His free hand roamed my body, feeling the parts of me that had been forbidden all these years. He massaged my breast and shot painfully good jolts as he squeezed my nipple between his index and thumb. I couldn't help but cry out Derek's name, his cock stretching me out exactly the way I needed to be filled. As expert fingers rubbed teasing circles on my clit, I could feel my climax build up.

My hips grinded against his hand, needing to feel more of him. Within seconds of rougher treatment, a powerful orgasm began heating me from my core, spreading throughout my body. I buried my face into his pillow, not wanting to wake anyone in the house with my moans. Derek took the opportunity to stop fingering me at just the right time, holding onto my curves as he let me ride out the explosive waves on his cock. Tremors racked my body as I recovered from my orgasm, and Derek pulled me to my knees, flipping me around so that I was on my stomach. With a hand under my chin, he urged me up into a kneeling position. I shuddered when I felt his hands smooth down my back, and I felt the light brush of his lips as they followed his hands. He pressed his chest against my back and grabbed my breasts, sending surges of pleasure through me. "Feel what you do to me, Karla," he moaned into my ear.

Derek swirled the head of his cock around my entrance, inadvertently dragging my sensitive clit against him. I moaned in pleasure. A hand threaded through my hair, pulling my head back as I arched in pleasure. I could feel the groan on his lips as he pulled me closer to him.

In one swift movement, he plunged himself into me, making me cry out as he buried himself to the hilt inside me. I could feel my pleasure building up again.

"Derek," I gasped out. "I'm going to...I'm going to cum again."

A deep groan rumbled through him, his cock twitching inside me, and I knew he was close as well. He started groaning my name more and more, almost chanting it. Letting go of my hair, he moved to grab my waist and continued to build up to our release. I wanted to see his face as he came, so I ran my fingers through my hair and pulled my head back until we were face-to-face. His eyes were shut tightly, and his jaw was clenched in concentration. He was the most gorgeous thing I'd ever seen. I squeezed my pussy around him and he threw his head back, groaning out my name and cumming hard. The warmth of his seed filled me, and I let out a moan of pleasure as I reached my own climax, my body shuddering with the force of my release. He collapsed onto me as we both rode out the last of our pleasure.

We laid quietly for awhile, catching our breaths and enjoying the afterglow. Derek kissed the back of my neck and I could feel the smile on his lips. He looked down at me affectionately. "I love you, Karla."

I looked up into his eyes and smiled as his arm curled around my waist, drawing me into him. I was drained in the most delicious way, physically and emotionally. All that was left to do was nuzzle myself into his chest and drift off into a blissful slumber.

9

I awoke to a tickling on my arm. Blinking my eyes open, I was met by a grinning Derek drawing a heart on my hand with a Sharpie.

He won.

"Hey!" I exclaimed, flicking at the Sharpie. "Not fair, I was asleep."

Chuckling, he responded, "Let's be real, Karla. I could've killed you a hundred times already."

"How long have I been your target?"

"Since the beginning."

Oh.

"Let's head out and grab brunch? You've been out for a while... I guess I really knocked you out, huh?" The last was said with a wink, and I felt heat blossom to my cheeks.

Avoiding his burning gaze, I glanced at the crumpled pile of purple silk on the ground then back at Derek. "I can't go anywhere wearing that."

Derek pulled his office chair towards us; on it was one of my sundresses, folded neatly with fresh panties and a bra. "You don't have to," he said with a grin.

"Where did you get this?" I asked, gaping at my clothes. Shrugging, he explained that he had sent his Little Brother to the TBM house for me. I smiled appreciatively at avoiding the walk of shame.

Slipping into fresh clothes, I ran my fingers through my tangled hair. When I was done smoothing out stray strands, Derek gave me an apprehensive smile, holding out a hand.

"Come on. We have a bit to talk about."

The Uber dropped us off outside of a sleek, contemporary building, where modern design seamlessly blended with timeless elegance. Puzzled, I got out of the car, glancing at Derek to see if we had come to the wrong place. He seemed at ease.

Why are we at the country club?

Confidently, Derek took my hand, maneuvering us past groups of people, effortlessly acknowledging and exchanging greetings with those who clearly recognized him. I couldn't help but cast a curious glance at him, wondering how he had become so acquainted with the affluent crowd, considering our parents were far from wealthy.

Without hesitation, he led me into a stunning glass house, acknowledging the hostess with a nod of familiarity before guiding us to a table adorned with exquisite gold and white decorations.

"Derek, what are we doing here?" I hissed while smiling at the waitstaff, pretending I belonged.

In a moment, the waitress arrived, presenting us with mimosas and a platter adorned with an array of delicacies, including smoked fish, caviar, cuts of meat, and an assortment of cheeses. A separate platter held scones, crackers, and other carb-filled goodness. *There's no way I can afford this,* I thought, but Derek's unwavering composure reassured me.

"If you require anything else, Mr. Sawyer, please do not hesitate to let me know." She waited for Derek's dismissal before leaving.

I waited until she was out of earshot before I said anything.

"Okay. What's going on?" I was on the verge of breaking into a fit of giggles. "Is this a joke? Why does everyone know you? Why is she talking to you like that?"

"You first," Derek said, his voice low with a hint of danger, like he knew I was hiding something. I bit into a scone.

"What do you mean, me first?"

"You first with telling me the truth."

So maybe I shouldn't have made him sweat our relationship that *much... but this is ridiculous!* "I talked to my mom yesterday... Our parents broke up."

"And why didn't you tell me that sooner?" Derek's face was a mask, and I couldn't tell if he was pissed or not.

Sipping my mimosa for a burst of courage, I responded, "Because I wanted to make sure you were serious about me first ... That's all. *Really*, that's all." The suspicion on his face started to fade, and his lip turned up just the slightest bit, making my mouth water. "So, why does everyone know you?" I asked, unable to look away from his kissable lips.

"I own this club."

I almost spat out my mimosa. "What do you mean… Own it? When? How?"

"I mean everything here is funded by me. If you want to get technical, I've bought out all of the country clubs in the state." Derek watched my face carefully as if to see if I already knew.

My eyes were bulging, I knew it, but I couldn't help it; not when Derek was blowing my mind.

"How the—" I exclaimed, lowering my voice when heads turned our way. "How the fuck did you manage that?" I whispered loudly.

"When I got accepted into Twin Peaks Uni, one of my classmates hooked me up with a job as the stable boy to help pay for the tuition and, later, the fraternity fees."

His blue eyes flicked to the wall, and I followed his gaze to where a portrait hung. The man in the portrait was familiar. Suddenly, I remembered him from the Mu Beta Alpha house. My jaw dropped.

Derek continued, "I ended up helping out as much as I could outside of my actual duties, working overtime. The owner really liked that. Always tried to get his grandson—my classmate—to do what I did, but he wasn't interested. He had enough money to not care about working overtime." Derek paused to sip his mimosa. "Long story short, I spent a lot of time learning from him. He fathered me the way my own dad neglected to... Sadly he passed away late last year. To my surprise, he left this club in my name in his will. From there, it spiraled. Things went so well that I was able to buy out all of the other ones."

"Why are you still in school? Why didn't you tell me earlier? Do mom and dad—your dad, I mean—know?"

Derek shook his head. "Well, yes and no. None of the brothers know, and I'd like to keep it that way because otherwise, they'll leech. Although, as you saw, the MBA brothers are not pleased. Your mom doesn't know, from my understanding. My dad, however, does know. How did you think you got your tuition and sorority dues paid for?"

I nodded, my head swimming. It was so much to take in at once. Our parents weren't together. Derek was rich beyond my imagination. My sisters liked me. Derek liked me. *He loved me.*

"You okay?" he asked, concern shining in his eyes as my pupils dilated.

"It's just… a lot. Wow. Thank you, by the way, for my tuition," I added with a nervous laugh. Derek chuckled, fluttering his fingers like it was nothing.

When we were done eating, Derek tugged at my hand.

"Come on, I'll teach you how to ride a horse. There's a pretty sweet spot hidden by the mountains that I've been wanting to take someone special to for a while."

"Hidden?"

"Yeah," he winked. "Lots of privacy for…"

Oh. I felt myself grow hot. I picked up my pace, letting him guide me to his horse. Suddenly, I felt happier than I'd ever been. What the future would bring, I didn't know, but it was going to be perfect.

Also by Stephanie Brother

Have you read the books in the Amazon Bestselling Huge Series?
HUGE | HUGE X 2 | HUGE X3 | HUGE X4 | HUGE 3D | HUGE STEPS | 10 MEN
HUGE X10 | HUGE PLAYERS | HUGE F-BUDDIES | TEAM PLAYERS | HUGE HOUSE HATES

Have you checked out the new spin-off Beyond Huge Series
HUGE DARE | HUGE DEAL

Have you read books in the Multiple Love Series?
BIG 3 | HOT 4 | HARD 5 | DEEP 6 | STEEL 7 | INKED 8 | CLOUD 9 | 10 INCHES

Other Contemporary Romances

[BILLION DOLLAR DADDY](#) | [BILLION DOLLAR STRANGER](#) | [BILLION DOLLAR SECRET](#)
[BIG D](#) | [MR. OMG](#) | [ARRESTED](#) | [LAWLESS](#) | [STEPBROTHER X3](#) | [FORBIDDEN X4](#)

***

Email me at
Stephaniebrotherbooks@hotmail.com

Excerpt from BIG 3

1

I'm not sure what is worse: finding out that Nate is a cheater or having to pack to leave him while he watches. There's so much shame in discovering that the pathetic feelings you had were all just an illusion, and even more shame in realizing the man you thought you loved is an asshole.

"Why are you so dramatic about this? Did you seriously think that we were exclusive?" Nate's face curves into a sly smile that sets the hairs on my arms raising. Oh God. Why didn't I see this side of him before my heart got involved? Why didn't I realize that he was deceitful and cruel? He charmed and flattered me into this relationship for what? So he could stick his dick into anything that moved while pretending to be the perfect boyfriend. I don't even know what else to say.

"You called me your girlfriend." My voice is high pitched and raised, which only makes him smile more.

"Well, you are, Natalie," Nate says slowly as though he thinks I'm too stupid to grasp words spoken at a normal rate. "The other girls...well, they're just there for the physical side. To do the things you won't do."

I grit my teeth as I toss the last of my clothes into the suitcase. Nate's eyes follow me from where he's lounging against the doorjamb. Of course, this is all my fault. Just because I wouldn't let him stick his dick in my ass, is that seriously how he's going to justify his constant infidelity? I've given this man a year of my life. My photographs have turned his travel blog from third-rate to go-to. I'm what's catapulted his income from subsistence hostel level to five-star. And this is what I get for my efforts? He hasn't paid me for any of it.

I guess he'd say that I've had the experience of a lifetime. He's supported all my living expenses for the entire time we've been traveling, but now I've seen what a lowlife he is, I'm walking away with nothing. Worse than that, I've had to call Mom to book me a flight home.

There are a million things that I could tell him right now, but I don't have it in me to try and argue with a man who will never accept he's in the wrong.

"You can't expect me to be satisfied with just this." He waves his hand across the room, as though our life together has been so boring to him. "We're not married. This is the time for us to experience everything we can before we settle down together."

"Settle down. You seriously think that I'd want to settle down with you, knowing what you've done." Of course, Nate didn't share our open-relationship status with me. I had to find it out from a well-meaning waitress who'd seen Nate with three women in the past week. I'd been telling her all about what an amazing boyfriend he was for buying me a silly necklace, and she took pity on me. She'd gone through something similar herself and couldn't stand to see another rat-bastard (her words) get away with it. Thank goodness. This charade could have gone on and on. Would he ever have been honest?

No. I know that for sure.

His lies gave him something to hold over me. I was loyal to him, and he wouldn't have wanted it any other way. As if he would have accepted me fucking other men. I think about the men I've met on our travels, back to Marley and his smooth brown skin and amazing physique. He'd liked me. I'm pretty certain of that. We could have had amazing sex. He had hands big enough to crush Nate's stupid head like a nut. Hands big enough to hold me while he fucked me against one of the palm trees on the beach in Jamaica. Or Marco. That man had liquid chocolate eyes and a smooth Italian accent that could slide the panties from even the most uptight of women. He was a charmer for sure, but I bet he would have been passionate between the sheets.

So many men. So many missed opportunities.

And how would Nate have compared? There's no way he would ever have accepted me discovering that his dick was smaller or his body less toned. Orgasms have been few and far between recently, as though he's given up caring about my pleasure. He's become lazy as his cheating has increased.

Well, fuck him. Fuck all men who think they can have their cake and eat it too.

"I have the ring," he says. "It's in the nightstand. Take a look."

"What?"

"The ring," he says again slowly, and I want to punch him in the face. I'm not looking anywhere except in the bathroom for my make-up bag. I'm out of here. He can give his lying, cheating ring to one of his other women – the one who took it up the ass like the trooper that I'm definitely not.

"I don't want to look at a ring," I reply equally slowly. "My cab will be here in five minutes."

"Natalie." He shakes his head like a teacher who has caught a pupil eating candy in class. "Always the drama queen. Are you really going to go through with this? You know we have flights to Cambodia in two days. Just think about Angkor Wat and the spectacular shots you'll be able to take there. It's the chance of a lifetime."

"There'll be other chances," I say, but even as the words pass my lips, I don't believe them. I know what I'm walking away from, and it's killing me.

Tomorrow I'll be home with my tail between my legs, an empty bank account, and no job. Traveling around the world is going to be the last thing on my mind. This morning I was sitting on the balcony staring out at the swelling sea, filled with false hope. By tomorrow, I'll be back home to an uncertain future.

"Why give up this one?" He saunters into the room as though we're discussing which of the five hotel restaurants to eat in this evening, rather than the acrimonious end of our lives together. "I didn't know this is how you'd react. If I'd known…"

"You'd what?"

"I'd have talked to you…explained how important it is to me that we experience all aspects of pleasure together. If you'd accepted that…"

I put up my hand because I just don't want to hear any more bullshit. As though the universe is listening with my same disgust, the phone rings. It's Connie, and I couldn't be more relieved to see a friendly name pop across the screen.

"Hey, Connie," I say, turning my back on Nate and heading to the bathroom.

"Natalie. I got your message. Are you seriously coming home tonight?"

"Seriously," I say, kicking the door closed and holding the phone against my ear with a raised shoulder while I gather my toiletries.

"That's amazing. I can't wait to see you."

"Me too. It's been too long." It really has been. A year without my bestie has been tough. Yes, technology makes the world smaller, but video chats aren't the same as sitting on the same sofa and sharing a bottle of wine. I've missed my friend, and now that my heart is shredded, her warm words and kindness feel even more distant.

"I know your mom moved last September. How do you feel about moving in?"

"Okay, I guess. She's pretty much ordered me to live with her. There are about ten spare rooms for me to choose from, and the house is right on the beach."

"That'll be perfect. You can sun yourself while you get used to being on home ground."

"No rest for me," I say. "I'll need to find work straight away."

"I'm sure something will come up, and in the meantime, let your rich stepfather put his hand in his pocket." Connie chuckles evilly. Conrad Banbury is richer than Croesus. The house I'm going to be staying at temporarily is just one of many, and worth well over fifteen million big ones. I guess he can afford to keep me for a while, but it's not something I'd feel comfortable with at all. I mean, I've only met the man once before I left the U.S. with Nate, and that was a rushed brunch where Mom laughed nervously and fluttered her hands too much.

"Conrad has generously paid for my flight home. I think that's about all I'm okay with him doing."

"I should think so too. He probably found the money for the ticket down the back of his designer couch."

"Probably."

"So, let's meet for lunch on Wednesday. My treat."

"Sounds good. My diary is wide open." I blink quickly as tears spring to my eyes. The amazing itinerary that I'd planned out with Nate is now an unfulfilled dream. Once I'm back in the States, my passport will find its way back into a dusty drawer.

"We'll go to that taco place you love. And for ice-cream sundaes after, okay?" I can hear how desperately Connie is trying to make my return less painful.

"That sounds great." My response is only half honest.

We say our goodbyes, and I inhale deeply before I tug the door open. Nate is relaxing in one of the plush teal velvet bucket seats, one leg resting on the other knee like a bored celebrity. His eyes are fixed to his phone, so I ignore him and stuff my toiletry bag into my bulging case. Sweat pricks at my armpits and my upper lip despite the air-conditioning.

It takes so much force to close the case that I'm out of breath by the time I'm done. All I need to do now is check the room and my travel documents and get my purse packed for the journey. There's a hollow and shaky feeling in my chest and heat on my cheeks that is only partially related to how hot I am. Doing this with Nate's eyes on me is just the final humiliation.

"Natalie. Just sit down for a minute," he says, waving to the matching vacant chair next to him. "You look like you're struggling, and we should talk. This is all very hasty."

"I'm not going to sit down." I glance around the room, spotting my phone charger and my camera's charge pack on the ornate desk. Two things I'd be lost without. There's a bottle of water there too, and I snag it for my purse. By the time I'm done here, I'm going to need a quenching drink – something to wash away the bitter taste in my mouth. The room's phone starts to ring, and I know it's reception notifying me of the arrival of my airport transfer. Nate's expression darkens as he realizes this whole situation is about to come to an end. He's about to lose control. All of his pretense at calm is wiped away that second, and I get a glimpse of how he really feels. It isn't pretty.

After I've told reception I'll be down in a minute, I feel even more frantic. While Nate was all smooth words and relaxed gestures, I was okay. Now, something in my gut is telling me things could get ugly.

I toss the strap to my purse over my shoulder, grab my camera bag, and heft my suitcase onto the pristine white tiled floor. It makes such a loud thud that Nate's shoulders rise and his face contorts.

"NATALIE."

My heart accelerates, the pounding echoing through the emptiness behind my ribs. My feet propel me toward the door, not looking to see if Nate has stood from his chair. I fumble with the handle but manage to get it open and shove my case into the corridor. Two businessmen are walking past, and I'm grateful to fall behind them, hoping that Nate won't make a scene when he has an audience. At the elevators, I chance a look back at the room and see the man who's been my life for too long standing with his arms folded, watching me walk away.

How many hours did we spend together, hours that I will never get back? How can someone who was everything to me yesterday be nothing to me today?

As the elevator doors close, all the effort it took to hold myself together suddenly feels too much. My shoulders slump, and my chest hitches, squeezing a sob from my throat that elicits glances from the others standing around me.

Shit.

I can't make a scene. I don't want people's eyes on me, or their pity. It's just another layer of humiliation. Another deep breath forces down the swell of misery and disappointment.

I can do this. I can make it home.

And once I'm there, I'll have to force myself to move on because there really is no other way. Who knows what lays in store for me?

A blank page.

It's a scary thought. But I know one thing for sure. No man is ever going to have the chance to make a fool of me this way again. My shattered heart is getting put into a metal box and locked away. I won't be an idiot twice.

2

There's a pristinely uniformed limousine driver waiting for me in the airport with my name in ornate cursive. Natalie Monk. As soon as I read it, I remember how Nate used to snigger any time someone would call my name. Funny that I was never conscious of it before, but now it feels weird to see it written so boldly.

"Hi, that's me," I say, nodding at the sign.

The round-faced man smiles and puts the sign under his arm, reaching for my suitcase. "I'm Daryl. You get stuck in immigration?"

"I think it was just backed up."

I follow him out of the terminal building to a ridiculously long car, which is more luxurious than anything I've ever ridden in. As Daryl puts my luggage in the trunk, I slide into the cavernous interior, marveling at the soft leather seats and shiny walnut trim. There's even a section for drinks and glasses, and I get a craving for a gin and tonic even though I'm completely shattered from the journey. I just need something to take the edge off, but I stop myself, instead retrieving a perfectly chilled bottle of water.

I don't think Mom would approve if I show up smelling of alcohol at this time of the day. She's probably already disappointed about what's happened. She really liked Nate. He had a way of flattering her subtly that impressed her a lot. I haven't told her what he did yet. It's too humiliating. All she knows is that we've broken up, and that's all I'll be sharing.

The drive toward the coast is scenic, but I'm so tired that I let my eyelids close and rest my head against the side of the vehicle, my mind battling with all the things I didn't say to Nate. An hour passes before the driver slows, pressing a buzzer, which jolts me from my tortured rest, and informing whoever is on the other end of the intercom that I've arrived.

Large iron gates open automatically, and the car makes its way up a long driveway on an upward incline. I guess the house is perched up high. That'll make the views spectacular.

Mom told me that they have a private beach. Imagine. This isn't the life I grew up with. Dad worked in a bank, and mom was a personal assistant in a big corporation. We lived in an everyday house with a regular car. When Dad passed away, Mom kept us going with Dad's life insurance. Then she met Conrad just over a year ago and everything changed.

I feel like an imposter when the driver opens the door for me, and I'm left to walk to the double-height doorway with just my purse as a shield. I have no idea what to expect.

What I get is my mom appearing at the door before I can even ring the bell.

"Natalie." She pulls me into a perfumed hug that doesn't feel familiar. She smells expensive, and the silk kaftan she's wearing is nothing like I've ever seen her in before. She's turned into a Stepford wife in my absence and I don't like it. Mom was the only familiar thing I had to return to and now she's different.

"Hey, Mom."

She draws back, gripping me by the shoulders with her manicured fingers, scanning me with overly made-up eyes. "You look thin."

I glance down at myself, even though I know I'm wearing baggy pants and a loose blouse that doesn't reveal anything of my body shape. Nate liked it when he could feel my hip bones. He was always telling me how pretty they were, and I've been so busy. It's hard to find time to eat when you're constantly on the move.

"And you look tired."

Wow, she's full of compliments today.

"It was a long flight." I smile as broadly as I can force because I don't need an argument on the doorstep. Especially after yesterday's misery.

"Natalie." Conrad appears in the wide hallway, dressed exactly the way you'd expect of a semi-retired millionaire, with a broad sparkling grin that probably cost fifty thousand dollars in veneers. "It's so good to have you home."

Home. That's a generous statement, bearing in mind I've never crossed this threshold before. I guess I should be grateful for the generosity and just put away my prickliness. "Thanks," I say. "For the flight and for letting me stay. It won't be for long."

"Don't be silly." Mom waves her arm in an expansive movement. "This house is huge. It's no trouble at all. Come. I'll show you to your room. I picked the best one with an ocean view to die for. I know how much you love the ocean. Really, it is the most spectacular place to live."

Conrad chuckles, putting his hands into the pockets of his tan slacks. "Your mom really loves it here." There's so much fondness in his expression that any doubts I had about his relationship with my mom fade a little. "I'll be in my office. Let me know what time dinner will be served."

Mom leads me up the glass-sided staircase, and we're followed by a man dressed in a shirt and formal black dress pants, who's appeared with my luggage. It's such an amazing home, with ridiculously high ceilings and softly colored chalky walls covered with expensive art. My sandals clap against the polished oak floors as we make our way down a long corridor. At the end, Mom opens a door to a room that exceeds the size and décor of any of the amazing hotels I've stayed in on my journeys, and that is saying something. But I'm not focused on the huge bed or the amazing silver crushed-velvet sofa for long. The room has bi-fold doors that open out onto a balcony overlooking the sea, and Mom is right. The view really is stunning.

"Wow," I say, dropping my purse on the bed and practically pressing my nose against the glass. Mom lifts the handle and slides the doors aside, and I'm caught in a breeze that smells of heaven. The shushing sound of the waves is like a balm to my tired mind. There is a small rattan sofa with light gray cushions on the balcony. I slump into it, unable to tear my eyes away from the turquoise of the ocean that spreads before me like an undulating blanket.

"It really is something special, isn't it," Mom says with a sigh. "You know, I wondered if I'd stop noticing the view after I'd been here for a few months, but I haven't. It still takes my breath away every day."

She takes a seat next to me and crosses her legs, resting her hands on her knees. "I'm glad you're home," she says. "I've been worried about you in all those places."

"I was always fine," I say. "But it's good to be back."

"So Nate is continuing on without you?" She's fishing for more information about what happened, but I don't blame her. I was very vague on the phone.

"Yes. He'll be in Cambodia tomorrow."

Mom screws up her nose but doesn't say anything. She's never been a traveler and doesn't have a concept of how vast and awe-inspiring the world really is. Countries that don't have the standards of development that she is used to aren't appealing to her in the slightest. "Well, I'm sure he's really going to miss you."

I know it's my fault that she's so in the dark about Nate, but her comment still stings. I imagine Nate convincing one of the other girls he's been fucking to join him on his trip. Maybe he'll buy her a camera and see if she can take some shots of the temples at Angkor. They won't be as good as mine would have been, but maybe he won't care as long as he can stick his dick where the sun doesn't shine.

"He'll be fine," I say, then decide to change the subject so that I don't get dragged into a debate. "I'm meeting up with Connie tomorrow. She's going to take me out for lunch."

"Well, that's just lovely. Something for you to do. Your stepbrothers won't be home for a couple of days, so you'll be stuck with Conrad and me for company."

"That's fine," I say. "It'll be good for us to catch up." Why she thinks I'm interested in the comings and goings of strangers, I've no idea. I wonder if she's forgotten that I've never met Conrad's sons. I'm sure she told me their names at some point last year, but I can't recall.

"So, what would you like to do now? Maybe take a nap...get rid of those dark circles?"

"Yes," I say. "That would be amazing."

"Then I'll come and wake you for dinner. And maybe a walk along the beach. You really have to see it up close."

"Perfect."

Mom reaches out to squeeze my leg. "Welcome home," she says, and I smile even though I know I'm going to sob into the pillows on the elaborately carved bed as soon as she leaves. Home is where the heart is, and I think I've lost mine somewhere between here and Bangkok.

About the Author

International bestselling author Stephanie Brother writes high heat love stories with a hint of the forbidden. Since 2015, she's been bringing to life handsome, flawed heroes who know how to treat their women. If you enjoy stories involving multiple lovers, including twins, triplets, stepbrothers, and their friends, you're in the right place. When it comes to books and men, Stephanie truly believes it's the more, the merrier.

She spends most of her day typing, drinking coffee, and interacting with readers.

Her books have been translated into German, French, and Spanish, and she has hit the Amazon bestseller list in seven countries.

Printed in Dunstable, United Kingdom